First published by Parragon in 2008

Parragon
Queen Street House
4 Queen Street
Bath BA1 1HE, UK

ISBN 978-1-4075-0875-7

Printed in China

That's Not My Mom!

Written by
PETER BENTLY

Illustrated by
JOHN BENDALL-BRUNELLO

PaRragon

Bath · New York · Singapore · Hong Kong · Cologne · Delhi · Melbourne

Gerry and Mom were out walking one day,
when a long line of termites
came marching their way.

Gerry watched as they all
crossed the path, one by one,
but when he looked up—
his mommy was
GONE!

"Lost your mom?" asked a sunbird.
"She's nearby, don't you worry!
The termites will show you
the way if you hurry."

"Where's my mom?"

So off Gerry galloped
in great leaps and bounds,
till he screeched to a halt
by some huge termite mounds.

"Aha!" Gerry cried.
"Now I'm on the right trail.
That definitely looks like
my mom's tufty tail!"

"That's not my mom!"

Gerry ran to the river
as quick as a flash.
There he saw something blinking
and heard a loud splash.

"Aha!" Gerry cried.
"Now what's that I spy?
That sounds like Mom drinking—
and look, there's her eye!"

"Lost your mom?" cackled Croc.
"Take a look over there.
I'm sure I saw something
with spotty brown hair."

A little way off,
Gerry heard a strange sound—
something was snoring
nearby on the ground!

ZZZZZ

"Aha!" Gerry cried,
as he peered through a gap.
"I'm sure that's my mom!
She's just taking a nap!"

"Lost your mom?" Leopard yawned.
"There's one place you could try.
In that baobab tree
I heard something up high."

"That's not my mom!"

Near the baobab tree
Gerry started to stare.
Was there something familiar
moving up there?

"Aha!" Gerry cried.
"That looks just like Mom's neck,
stretching up for some leaves.
I'll just go and check!"

"Lossst your mom?" whispered Snake.
"If she loves to chew,
there are nice tasssty leaves
in that clump of bamboo."

As he skipped up the hill
Gerry heard a loud MUNCH!
Some large chomping creature
was eating its lunch.

"Aha!" Gerry cried,
and he started to laugh.
"Who else could have feet like that
but a giraffe?"

"Lost your mom?" chuckled Zebra,
as he flicked off the flies.
"Go back to the woods,
and you'll get a surprise."

As Gerry came close
to the thick jungle glade,
he saw some giraffes
in the cool of the shade.

Then from the trees
came a voice soft and calm,
saying, "Hi, little guy!"
Gerry cried...

So Gerry and Mom,
in the shade of a tree,
had a BIG hug
that was snug as can be.

"Aha!" Gerry cried,
"I'm sure that's Mom's ear.
Bamboo is so tasty—
no wonder she's here!"

"Lost your mom?" rumbled Rhino,
looking over his shoulder.
"Did I see a giraffe
over there by that boulder?"

By now Gerry felt like he'd
been searching for hours.
But at last—what was standing
behind those bright flowers?